Ariel
Is My Babysitter

By Andrea Posner-Sanchez
Illustrated by Mario Cortés & Meritxell Andreu

 A GOLDEN BOOK · NEW YORK

randomhousekids.com

ISBN 978-0-7364-3446-1 (trade) — ISBN 978-0-7364-3447-8 (ebook)

Printed in the United States of America

10 9 8 7 6 5 4

One afternoon in Atlantica, Princess Ariel was ready to start her very first **babysitting job**.

"Goodbye," she called to Melvin Octopus's parents. "Have a good time at the party!"

"See you later!" added Melvin. He was looking forward to having fun with the little mermaid.

"What are we going to do?" Melvin asked.

"I heard there's a sunken ship not too far away," Ariel said. "Let's go **exploring**!"

"Cool!" said Melvin, and they set off.

As the **shipwreck** came into view, Ariel's eyes widened.

"Actual humans were once on this ship," she said in amazement.

Melvin didn't know what humans were, but he was just as excited!

"Ooh, what's that? And that? And that? And that? And that? And that? And that? And that?" Melvin asked, pointing in eight different directions at once.

"I wish I knew," Ariel said with a giggle.

The ship's steering wheel caught Ariel's eye. "I wonder what this does," she said.

Melvin rushed over to check it out. The thing had eight knobs—one for each of his tentacles. So he decided to climb on.

When Melvin had all of his tentacles on the wheel, it started **spinning**!

"Whoa! That was one crazy ride!"

Finally the wheel came to a stop. Ariel couldn't help laughing as the dizzy little octopus tried to swim straight.

Then Ariel noticed something **shiny** in the sand. "I'll get it out!" Melvin volunteered. He used his tentacles to dig and dig.

Before long, Melvin had uncovered a silver strainer.

"I have no idea what it is, but I love it!" Ariel declared.

"It's the coolest treasure I've ever seen!" Melvin said.

After all the excitement, it was time to go.

"It's almost bedtime," Ariel said. She took one of Melvin's tentacles in her hand and started to swim home. But she didn't get very far—Melvin had wrapped his other tentacles tightly around the ship's mast!

"I'm not ready to go home. I want to have more fun!" Melvin squirted a cloud of **ink** and took off. "Try to catch me!" he yelled as he swam away.

When the ink cleared, Ariel didn't know where to look.
Octopuses are good at hiding—they can change color
to blend in with their surroundings.

Ariel looked **this way**.

And Ariel looked **that way**. But she couldn't find Melvin.

Ariel zoomed through the seaweed forest.

She **zipped** around Sebastian's orchestra
practice. But she still couldn't find Melvin.

Out of breath, Ariel stopped to rest.

"I am the worst babysitter ever!" she mumbled to
herself. "Melvin's parents will be home soon, and I've lost Melvin!"

Then Ariel heard snoring. She looked down and saw Melvin! He had dug himself a hole and fallen fast asleep.

She used the silver strainer to gently scoop him out of the sand.

Melvin woke up and smiled. **"You found me!"** he said to Ariel. "You're a good babysitter."

Melvin was too sleepy to swim home, so Ariel carried him in the strainer. "I'll have to ask Scuttle if humans use this for carrying children around," she said.

Melvin was safe in bed just moments before his parents arrived.

"I hope Melvin didn't give you any problems," Mrs. Octopus said to Ariel.

"Oh, nothing I couldn't handle," Ariel replied.

It was one **babysitting adventure** she would never forget!